Best Friends
Forever

Best Friends Forever

Joyce Moyer Hostetter

Illustrated by Eddie Ross

Books are our BFFs!

Joyce M. Hostetter

FRIENDSHIP PRESS
New York

Editorial Offices:
475 Riverside Drive, New York, NY 10115

Distribution Offices:
P.O. Box 37844, Cincinnati, OH 45222-0844

99 98 97 96 95   5 4 3 2 1

Library of Congress Cataloging-in-Publication Data

Hostetter, Joyce.
   Best friends forever / Joyce Moyer Hostetter; illustrated by Eddie Ross.
     p.   cm.
   Summary: When Rhoda, a young Mennonite staying with her grandparents for a year, meets Nadia, a Ukrainian immigrant, they vow to be best friends until the day they die.
   ISBN 0-377-00297-6
   1. Mennonites--Fiction. 2. Ukrainians--Fiction.
3. Friendship--Fiction 4. Death--Fiction   I. Ross, Eddie, ill.
II. Title.
PZ7.H81125Be 1995   94-48741
                               CIP
                               AC

Manufactured in the United States of America

To Wendy and Ben
for listening to each chapter as I wrote it,
and especially for laughing and crying
in all the right places.

Author's Note

Thank you, Maria Bilous Schlick, for introducing me
to your delightful family.

Thanks to Iwan Bilous and the whole Bilous clan
who let me tag along to Bound Brook to honor your
beloved Tina. You treated me just like a member
of the gang.

Thanks to all my Ukrainian friends for sharing
your customs and all those delicious foods with me.

Back to you, Maria: thanks for being my friend.
I'll love you till the day I die!

Contents

The Hat With a Story

Kristen Keeler traced her finger over the quilted design on her mother's bed.

"Can I go to New Jersey with you?" she asked her mother.

"And leave Daddy and Jonathan here alone? They would miss you," her mother replied.

"But you need someone to keep you company," said Kristen.

Her mother pulled a raincoat out of the closet and laid it on the bed—just in case it was raining in Bound Brook, New Jersey.

"Well, I'm used to going to Bound Brook alone," she said. "I do it every year."

"But why?" asked Kristen.

"Well, this trip to New Jersey is special—I like to do it all by myself."

"Why do you go to New Jersey anyway?" asked Kristen.

Mother paused for a moment as if she didn't know how to answer that question. Then she said, "I guess you could say I go to see a friend."

"What's her name?"

Mother threw a bottle of sunscreen into her overnight bag—just in case it was sunny in Bound Brook, New Jersey.

Then she said, "Her name, my dear, is Nadia."

"Nadia! That's my middle name. Is she a little girl like me?"

"No, but when I met her she was just ten years old. And I was ten too."

"Was Nadia your very best friend?"

"As a matter of fact, yes. Nadia was my very best friend." Mother stopped putting clothes in the suitcase. She picked up her straw hat—the one with the sheer white scarves attached for tying it on. She folded the scarves into the hat three times. Then she unfolded the scarves and pulled them through her hand, watching them bunch up and smooth out as they slipped through her fingers.

Kristen had never noticed the magic in this hat. But now she saw that the hat could take her mother very far away. She sat still and waited for her mother to tell her about that other Nadia.

Suddenly Mother folded the scarves again and put the hat on top of the raincoat.

"Remind me to tell you about Nadia sometime," she said.

"Tell me now, Mother. Please tell me now," Kristen begged.

Kristen's mother packed a sweater in her suitcase just in case it was cool in Bound Brook, New Jersey. She started to shake her head but Kristen's pleading was too much for her to resist.

"Okay," she said. "I will. You should know about Nadia."

Mother picked up the hat with the scarves and put it on. She climbed onto the bed with Kristen and pulled her daughter into her arms. They sat there crosslegged on the cozy quilt.

Mother pulled the scarves down over her shoulders and over Kristen's shoulders too. They hung there like two pigtails and Kristen smoothed them out with her hands.

Then Mother and the hat with the scarves took Kristen all the way back to the first time she ever saw her friend, Nadia.

1

Because You Wear Pigtails

I saw Nadia Kuropas before I saw anyone in the classroom. She stood out from all the other fifth graders like a colored image in a black and white photograph. Which is sort of strange when you think about it—her being in color. She was so plain, just like me. That's why I noticed her.

Why hadn't Grammy told me there was another Mennonite in my class, I wondered. I looked at Grammy who was handing my birth certificate to the teacher. Grammy looked at the boys and girls and then turned to the teacher as if she hadn't even noticed the girl with the brown pigtails.

A redheaded boy on the front row noticed. He looked at me and then at the other girl and said, "Now Nadia has a twin."

The other children snickered. The girl with the pigtails put her nose in the air and refused to smile. She must be Nadia, I thought. I smiled at her but she looked away.

I knew right then she was going to be my best friend. I looked shyly around the room while Grammy told the teacher I would be living here in Snow Hill, Maryland with her and Grandpop for only one year.

The teacher introduced me to the class.

"Boys and girls, this is Rhoda Landis," she said.

The teacher said her name was Miss Shockley and she was very happy to have me. She gave me a seat in the back of the classroom. I liked that because the other children couldn't stare at me and I could stare at Nadia.

I watched her the whole time Miss Shockley was calling the roll. I watched her during the Pledge of Allegiance and even during the Lord's Prayer.

I decided for sure she was Mennonite during the Pledge of Allegiance because she only pretended to say it. I said the pledge even though Grammy had told me not to. She said our allegiance was to the kingdom of God, not to a human kingdom.

Anyone who had seen Grammy with her hair pulled back in a bun and her white net covering would know we were different. Anyone who took one look at my pigtails would know it too. But just to fool them I said the pledge loud and clear.

After the Lord's Prayer when we said Amen, Nadia touched her forehead with her thumb and two fingers, and then she touched her chest a few times.

She did it again when we said grace at lunch time. I asked her about it in the girls' bathroom when we washed our hands.

"What's that?" I asked and tried to do the same thing she had done.

At first I thought she wasn't going to answer me.

Finally she said, "That's not how you do it." Then she showed me how.

I practiced until I got it right.

"What is it?" I asked.

"It's the sign of the cross, silly. Don't you know anything?"

"Well, I know the Pledge of Allegiance," I said. "I guess you don't because you didn't say it."

"I didn't want to," she replied as she left the bathroom and lined up with the other students in the hall.

I stood behind her in line and stared at her pigtails. I couldn't help but reach out to touch them. She turned and I whispered in her ear. "You are a Mennonite aren't you?"

"What's that?" she asked.

I could see from the surprise on her face that she really didn't know. What a disappointment!

"Never mind," I said. I didn't tell her because if she weren't a Mennonite she would never understand.

"Why do you wear pigtails?" I asked.

"I'm Ukrainian. That's why." She said it loudly and some of the other kids around us snickered and mocked her.

I thought about that for a minute as I followed her and the others down the hall.

"Is that the name of your church?" I asked.

"No, silly. That's the name of my country."

"You mean you're not American?"

"I am if I want to be. But I don't. Baba doesn't want to be either. She's going back to Ukraine as soon as the Iron Curtain comes down. She didn't want to come here in the first place."

"Who's Baba? And why did she come?" I asked as I followed her to a table in the lunchroom. We opened our bagged lunches and started eating while the other children went through the cafeteria line.

"Baba is my grandmother. She came here to get away from communism. But when communism is gone, she's going back."

"You are a Mennonite, aren't you?"

"What makes her think communism will go?"

"It will—because every day she sends hateful thoughts to the communists and every church service she prays that the communists will die a bloody death."

"Well," I said. "My Grammy has a motto in her spare room that says 'Love Your Enemies.'"

Then I thought Nadia might not like me criticizing her Baba so I told her about the other motto in the living room, the one that says, "Prayer Changes Things."

"So maybe it will work," I said.

By now all the tables around us were filling up. Only our table had space. A tall skinny boy with a mop of yellow hair came through the line and looked for a place to sit. Finally he sat at our table but down at the other end.

Another boy, the redheaded one who snickered at me earlier, sat with him and said, "Look. The twins both packed their lunches. I guess they can't afford to eat in the lunchroom."

The tall one said to us, "You know you can get free lunches if you're poor."

Nadia's eyes flashed at that. She tossed her head and said, "You must be out of your mind! Ukrainians do not take handouts."

"Did you hear that?" the tall one said to the redhead. "Ukrainians do not take handouts."

Nadia was really mad now. She was so mad she spit out a long stream of words that I couldn't understand.

The boys pretended to be shocked and said, "There she goes again talking in gibberish!"

"What did you say?" I asked her.

She whispered in my ears what she told them but I would never repeat it. I was afraid something bad would happen to me if I ever talked like that.

"Guess I told them, didn't I?" She looked really proud of herself.

During social studies class after lunch I wondered if I should be Nadia's friend after all.

But when school was over there was Nadia on bus number 23. That was the one Grammy had told me to ride. Well, if we were going to ride the same bus, we might as well sit together. Nadia was sitting in an aisle seat all by herself.

"Are you going to let me sit with you?" I asked.

She shrugged and turned her legs toward the aisle to let me climb over and sit by the window.

"You're supposed to sit with your best friend," I said.

"Who says you're my best friend?" Nadia asked me.

"Well, do you have another best friend?"

She was quiet for a moment.

"Well, do you?"

"I don't have any friends." The way she said it I almost thought she was proud of it.

"But why?" I asked.

"Because, silly. I'm Ukrainian."

"Oh—well don't you want a friend?"

She was quiet for a minute. Then she asked, "Why do you want to be my friend?"

"Because you wear pigtails," I said.

Then Nadia laughed. "That is the silliest reason I ever heard," she said.

I was so relieved to hear her laugh. I laughed too.

"It's time for me to get off," she said as the bus slowed to a stop. The house at the other end of her lane was the same one I had seen from my bedroom window at Grammy's house. I looked across the road and sure enough there was Grammy's house. Nadia and I were neighbors!

"It's time for me to get off too," I said. I followed her onto the side of the road. The bus driver wouldn't leave until I had crossed over in front of the bus. But after it was gone, I yelled to Nadia.

"Look! We're neighbors. We have to be best friends!"

Nadia laughed and twirled around until her pigtails stood straight out.

She looked so funny. I put down my brand new books and twirled around too. My pigtails swirled around my head and slapped me in the face when I slowed down.

Nadia waved and headed for the little white house at the other end of her lane. I picked up my books and ran home, shaking my head so that my pigtails danced in front of me.

2

Baba and the Dead Dido

Nadia and I ate lunch together every day that week. On Friday, she said I should come play at her house on Saturday.

Saturday morning I was too excited to eat breakfast.

"Ach," said Grammy. "This is Grandpop's homemade scrapple. You'll hurt his feelings if you don't eat it."

I looked at Grandpop to see if his feelings were hurt. He put his head down on the green checked table cloth so all I could see was his gray head with the bald spot in the middle. He pretended to cry.

"I butchered my favorite pig to make this scrapple," he said. "I even used my secret recipe. If you don't eat it I might have to send you back home to your mom and dad."

I knew Grandpop was teasing but it did scare me a little. I missed Mom and Dad but I was just getting to know Nadia and I didn't want to leave before I went to her house. So I ate the scrapple.

Grammy and Grandpop were still trying to decide if I should go to Nadia's house.

"What do you think, Daddy?" Grammy asked. "We don't know them very well."

"Maybe we should know them," Grandpop said. "They've lived here for years and I've only greeted him at Farm Bureau meetings a few times. I guess we haven't been such good neighbors."

"Well," said Grammy. "We did take them a pie when they moved here but they couldn't speak English and we couldn't speak Russian and so we just didn't go back."

"Grammy," I said, "they're not Russian. They're Ukrainian."

"It's all the same thing," said Grammy.

"That's not what Nadia says. She gets mad when the other children call her Russian."

"It sounds like we should go meet this friend of yours," said Grammy. "Let's make a shoofly pie and take it to them. Are you going to help me?"

I jumped up. I was ready to get started.

Grammy let me roll out the pie crust and even pour the hot molasses in the bottom. I already knew how to pinch the edges of the crust because Mom always let me do that at home.

When the pie was finished Grammy sent me to the barn to tell Grandpop we were ready. Before I got to the long low barn, I could hear the grunts of the pigs. And I could smell them even before I left the house. All the male pigs were out in the field. At Grandpop's house you could never get away from the smell of pigs.

Grandpop had a few cows, two goats and about twenty chickens, but mostly he just had pigs. I wished he had horses.

On Nadia's farm there were mostly chickens. She said her Batko (that's what she called her daddy) had 20,000 chickens. She was serious too. I asked her how you could gather the eggs from 20,000 chickens.

She said, "Don't be silly. These chickens don't lay eggs. We just raise them for eating."

"How can you eat that many chickens?" I asked her.

"Now that is ridiculous," she said. "We ship them to a poultry plant to get butchered and then they go to the grocery stores."

I could see Nadia's two chicken houses as Grammy, Grandpop and I walked down the long lane to her house. I wondered how 20,000 chickens could live in two houses but Nadia said they did.

It was cool, which Grandpop said was strange for so early in September. The ground was wet from the rain the night before and the world smelled like it had just been washed. I wanted to run the whole way to Nadia's house.

Nadia's one story white house was sheltered by three huge willow trees in the yard. A man and a woman were coming out of one of the chicken houses. I guessed they must be her Mama and Batko.

Nadia must have been watching for me because she came running out to greet us.

She introduced Batko and Mama to us. Batko smiled a huge smile at Grandpop and shook his hand. You could tell he felt they were friends just from saying hello at those Farm Bureau meetings.

Mama smiled and nodded and smiled some more at Grammy. When Grammy gave her the shoofly pie she grinned so big her eyes became little slits in her round face.

I looked at those two women standing there in the lawn and thought they looked almost the same. They each wore a sweater with only one button fastened over their fat bodies. Both wore a scarf tied under the chin. You couldn't even tell Grammy was a Mennonite with that scarf on. It would be easy to pretend she was Ukrainian. I decided to pretend we were all Ukrainian.

Grandpop didn't look like a Ukrainian or a Mennonite. He just looked like a man. Mennonite men didn't have to dress differently from other people. It just didn't seem fair.

It was hard to pretend I was Ukrainian when I could not understand a word Nadia's Mama was saying. Nadia translated for her.

"Come into the house," she said. "I will make coffee and we will talk."

She talked fast. She talked a lot. She told Grammy and Grandpop how happy they were that Nadia had a friend. For five years of school Nadia had not made one friend.

Nadia's Mama and Batko looked at me with so much love in their eyes I could feel it wrap around me and it didn't matter at all that I couldn't understand a word they said.

Mama explained why the children at school were not friendly to Nadia. "The children think she is a Russian," she said. "But we are not Russian!"

Batko shook his head. He agreed with her on that.

From the next room I heard a hissing sound. I didn't realize anyone was in there but then I remembered Baba, Nadia's grandmother who hated the communists.

When the coffee was ready Mama cut Grammy's shoofly pie and served it to everyone. Not only that. She handed around a big tray of triangle shaped fruit pies. "Piroschky," she said proudly. I ate three of those piroschky things because I figured I could eat shoofly pie just about anytime but I might not get another chance to eat Ukrainian food.

Nadia was kept busy translating for everyone. She

explained for my Grammy why I was living with them. Grammy said my mother had just had a baby and was having woman troubles. It got quiet then and I knew they would change the subject as soon as they could think of something else to say.

That's when Batko started to talk. He told all about their trip across the ocean. They had come because a man had promised them they could be free and get rich in America.

But when they got to America the man made them work from dark in the morning to dark at night. He would take them to the store but it was his store and he charged very high prices. Not only that, he made them pay high rent for the house they lived in. It was like they were the slaves and he was the owner.

"But Ukrainians are smart," said Mama. "No one will make us slaves. We saved enough money to send my husband's brother to Ohio. When he earned enough money in the factory there, he sent for us and we moved there too. My husband earned good money in the factory but I didn't like the city. So we moved back here and bought this house. Batko built the chicken houses with no help from contractors."

Bakto nodded his head. "I came to America for freedom," he said, "not for slavery."

I looked around the simple farm kitchen and into the living room next door. There were pictures of Jesus and Mary on the living room walls and each of them was draped with a lacy fabric. I wondered what the lace was for.

When my mind came back to the conversation I realized the adults had run out of things to say. Batko said we should meet Baba. We all followed Batko into the next room.

Baba was dozing in a chair in the corner.

Baba was dozing in a chair in the corner. On her lap was a bit of embroidered lace she'd been working on. Her head had fallen against the side wing of the chair and her mouth hung open as she slept. She had about a thousand wrinkles in her face.

I was sure I'd never seen such an old person in my life even counting all the old women who sat on the right hand side of my church in Pennsylvania. Not even counting old Mrs. Clemmer who gave me a mint life-saver every Sunday. Mrs. Clemmer was so old I some-times thought she might die before she could get the lifesaver out of the rolled up handkerchief in the cape of her dress.

I wondered how long it would take this ancient woman to find a lifesaver. I found out soon enough that Baba was a lot quicker than she looked.

She woke up the moment Batko called her name. She greeted each of us with grunts and frowns. Grammy and Grandpop just smiled and shook her hand. She grunted some more and I thought my grandparents were sure getting a chance to practice what they preach about loving their enemies.

I shook the old woman's papery hand. Then I sat on a green chair in the corner of the room.

Old Baba shrieked at me when I sat there. I didn't understand a word she said. But Nadia was quick to translate.

"Over here," she said. "Baba says, 'Can't you see Dido is sitting there?' She says you are very rude to sit where someone else is sitting." Nadia pulled me to the couch to sit with her. My heart was making such huge noises in my chest I was sure the old woman would yell at me to keep it quiet. I hung onto Nadia's arm for secu-rity. Suddenly I really did miss my mother and the comfort of Mrs. Clemmer's mint flavored lifesavers on Sunday mornings.

Baba talked and talked about Dido. Slowly I realized Dido had been her husband. But he had died in a work-camp in Siberia before Nadia and her family came to America on a boat.

Baba hissed and spat out a string of Ukrainian words that Nadia did not translate. I could only imagine what she said.

Grammy and Grandpop nodded sympathetically and I just huddled deeper into the couch and wondered what Mom and Dad were doing this morning. Then I remembered that Mom was too weak to do anything special.

She couldn't do much besides take care of my new baby brother. Still, I would even be willing to do dishes for her if I didn't have to sit here drowning in this strange language, wondering if the dead Dido might show himself to me too.

But I knew my older sisters were at home to help Mom. And I was here because I wasn't really such a good helper.

Of course I had wanted to come. Anyone would want to live with Grammy and Grandpop Kulp. Grammy loved to spoil her grandchildren and Grandpop was a wonderful tease.

And now I had met Nadia so what more could I need?

But I hadn't been prepared for Baba. I didn't like this strange woman who screamed at little girls and talked about a dead man as if were alive. Did she really believe he was there in that chair? Was he really in that chair?

I decided Baba must hate me as much as she did the Russians. She stared at me with her milky blue eyes as she told horrible stories about the concentration camp. She and Dido had been sent there because they dared to speak against the communists. For some reason the communists let her go home but Baba said they killed her Dido.

Nadia translated the stories with great pleasure. I could see she was proud of all the trials Baba had endured. She acted like Ukrainians were the only people in the world who had ever experienced persecutions.

Well, I decided right then and there I would bring Grandpop's *Martyr's Mirror* with me the next time. I didn't know how I would lug the huge book out Grandpop's long lane and down Nadia's, but I'd figure something out.

I didn't have to worry. Grandpop took care of that. First he asked Mama and Batko where they go to church. They said they went to the Ukrainian church but they didn't have services every Sunday. That was because the Ukrainian priest had to come all the way from Baltimore to conduct the services.

So Grandpop invited them to attend the Mennonite church with us. Baba answered for them. I thought the old woman had fallen asleep again, but even if she was old there was nothing wrong with her hearing.

She said they couldn't come to our church because the Kuropas family was Orthodox. In fact, said Baba, all Ukrainians were Orthodox and that was the way it was supposed to be.

Grammy said that her cousin in Canada had married a Mennonite from the Ukraine.

"I'm sure some Ukrainians are Mennonite," Grammy said.

Baba just hissed at that.

When Batko and Mama walked Grammy and Grandpop out into the yard later they said that sometimes Nadia could go to church with us. But she would go to the Orthodox church whenever they had services.

Grammy and Grandpop smiled and I knew they felt they had just won a soul for the kingdom of heaven.

Nadia walked over to our house the next morning to get a ride with us to church. I was glad she was early. I wanted to show her the pictures of the Mennonites who had been killed for their faith.

We didn't have time to look at many of the pictures in the big book but I showed her my favorites anyway. They made me feel just terrible because I knew the people being thrown into the rivers and burned alive were my ancestors.

I knew if we would have communism in our country we might have to die for our faith too. I was pretty sure I would never be able to die for God. I couldn't even stand it when the mean boys at my school in Pennsylvania pulled my pigtails and called me Amish.

But I could tell Nadia was impressed with the way the Mennonites had suffered and that made being different almost a good thing. Besides, Nadia was different too.

3

Scared Chickens

Every Saturday I went to Nadia's house to play. Every Sunday she came to my house and most Sundays she went to church with us too.

At Nadia's house our favorite place to play was in the large willow tree on the back lawn. Its long hanging branches made a green walled kingdom where Nadia and I were the queens. We usually took turns, but sometimes if we were feeling selfish we would both be queens, with Nadia on one side of the grand tree and me on the other.

But that didn't work because we'd get bossy and speak too loudly. We had a rule in our kingdom that we always spoke in whispers so the enemy wouldn't hear us.

The enemy was everybody else, especially Baba who thought little girls shouldn't climb trees. She tried to teach us ladylike things like making tatted lace.

I was too frightened to learn anything from Baba. Once when she tried to teach me, she got so angry she threw my tatting tool across the room and told us to go away from her.

"Let's go over to Grammy's house," I said.

"Take this varenyky with you," said Mama. She was always sending delicious Ukrainian foods to Grammy.

We ate the varenyky—delicious dumplings stuffed with potato and cheese—as soon as we got to Grammy's house. Grandpa pulled his harmonica from his pocket and played "What a Friend We Have in Jesus." I forgot all about Baba and her temper after that. So we went back to Nadia's house.

"Take some of my chicken corn soup to Mama and Batko," said Grammy. She dipped the soup into a two-quart jar and sent us on our way.

The good thing about Baba getting so angry was she never tried to teach us anything ladylike again. She mostly left us alone.

We always told Mama and Batko when we were going to our kingdom. Then we'd dash past the chicken houses and down to the creek. We'd circle back around and sneak through the thorny bushes that made a hedge around the yard.

We were proud of ourselves for making everyone think our kingdom was so far from the house instead of right there in the backyard dangerously close to the wicked Baba.

Of course Nadia never called her Baba wicked. She adored her grandmother and wasn't frightened by her at all.

I never called Baba wicked either. I just thought it. I tried not to because I was afraid she would send the dead Dido to visit me. But sometimes I just couldn't help what I thought.

One Saturday morning we were playing in the willow kingdom when we heard a car blowing its horn as it came in Nadia's long lane.

From our thrones in the willow tree we heard Batko yelling as he came out of the house.

"It's Uncle Walter," said Nadia. "He always blows the horn and upsets the chickens. Now Batko is swearing at him. Uh oh, he's calling our names. We'd better go."

Nadia and I scrambled out of the tree and dashed out of the kingdom. We backtracked through the hedge and down to the creek. By the time we reached the chicken house Batko was waiting for us.

"Go scatter the chickens," said Batko. "Your fool uncle is going to kill all my chickens yet. He will never stop blowing that horn!"

Nadia always remembered to translate everything Batko said so I would understand. She argued with her father in Ukrainian and remembered to tell me what she said too.

"But Batko, we want to see Uncle Walter and Aunt Helen too. Why do we have to scatter the chickens?"

"Go do it. Your uncle and aunt will be here when you are finished."

Batko turned toward the yard where Mama greeted the man and woman who had arrived in the shiny blue car. Nadia led me into the first chicken house.

She ran to the other end of the chicken house where all the chickens were scrambling to get away from the noise.

"If we don't scatter them they will trample each other to death," she said.

I did what Nadia did—running toward the flock of chickens waving my arms and yelling "Tikai, tikai!" I hoped that wasn't a swear word.

The chickens flew, ran, and clucked their way around me. They made a noise worse than a thousand people speaking a foreign language. I covered my face with my

I did what Nadia did—running toward the flock . . .

hands, wishing for more hands to hold my nose and cover my ears. The air was thick with flying feathers and the smell of chicken poop.

I wanted to get away from those chickens. But we still had one more house to go into.

The bright sunlight blinded me for a second as we stepped out of the first house. Then I was really in the dark when we went into the next one. I stood there trying to see where I should go but when Nadia yelled at me to come on, I followed her.

"Tikai, tikai!" I yelled with her. I hung to the back of the chickens this time, cringing as 10,000 white feathered squawkers surrounded me.

In the confusion I bumped into something and fell. I scrambled up from the thick carpet of chicken poop as fast as I could. I saw that I'd run into one of the watering troughs. It lay on its side and the water began to form a puddle all around it.

Nadia was calling my name.

"Hurry! Uncle Walter and Aunt Helen always bring presents. Hurry!"

I took one last look at the puddle of water and the goopy mess it was making in the chicken manure. Then I headed for the beam of light where Nadia stood at the chicken house door.

Nadia helped me wash up at the spigot outside. We got my dress wet trying to clean it up. But we decided I was clean enough to get presents so we went on inside.

Everyone was gathered in the living room around Baba, who was the mother of Uncle Walter as well as Batko. No one was sitting in the green chair in the corner and I didn't go close to it.

Nadia's Uncle Walter passed around a box of chocolates. Then he gave the rest to Nadia and told her to share it with me.

Baba began to tell Walter how his father had suffered in the concentration camp. Only the way she said it was like it was really Dido talking, saying things like, "I hated the guard with the scar on his lip. He hated me too, more than anyone in the camp. He was the one who killed me. He thinks no one knows who did it. But I know. And I won't forget it."

Uncle Walter talked right back to his father as though he believed he were really there. Aunt Helen didn't say much unless Baba told her to. I tried to look invisible so she wouldn't make the dead man talk to me but I think she had decided I wasn't worth noticing anymore.

After a while she waved everyone away and went to sleep.

Even though Baba was still in the room, I wasn't so afraid of her now. As long as she was asleep, she wouldn't be talking in the voice of dead people.

Nadia remembered the chocolates from Uncle Walter. As she shared them with me she and Aunt Helen decided to teach me some Ukrainian words. We were having a wonderful time until Batko came from the chicken house in a rage.

I didn't have to understand Ukrainian to know he was swearing at Nadia. I could see Nadia didn't know what she'd done wrong. I was afraid to ask. Aunt Helen put her arm around me and Nadia, and tried to calm everyone down.

"Stop yelling!" she said to Batko in English. "They are only children. I'm sure it was an accident. No harm done. Leave them alone."

Then Batko yelled at her. I felt sorry for her but I guess I didn't need to because she had a little smile on her round face.

Later when Nadia walked me home, I found out what

had happened. It was all my fault. The watering thing in the chicken house had flooded the place. Batko said if he lost 10,000 chickens to pneumonia it would be Nadia's fault.

The fear in my tummy felt like when Baba yelled at me. It wasn't Nadia's fault at all. It was my fault. Did Batko know that?

Nadia said not to worry—she'd let him believe it was her fault. She said Batko wouldn't believe it was me anyway. He thought I was perfect.

Nadia's punishment was to help feed the chickens for a whole week.

Nadia said, "Don't worry. Aunt Helen will help me with the chores."

But I did worry. I worried about whether 10,000 chickens would die. I worried about how relieved I felt to let Nadia take the blame.

Nadia said she should take the blame because she was the one who hurried me out of the chicken house to get Uncle Walter's presents. And anyway, how was I supposed to know the water would just keep running?

She made me feel a little better. But it felt even better to get back to Grammy and Grandpop's peaceful kitchen. The house smelled like chocolate chip cookies and Grammy said I could have one.

At supper that night, Grandpop read from the book of Isaiah before he said the blessing on the food.

I asked him what it meant when it said, "The chastisement of our sin was upon him." Grandpop said it meant Jesus had taken our sins so we wouldn't have to be punished.

When I thought of Nadia feeding chickens all next week when really I should be doing it, I knew exactly what he was talking about. While Grandpop thanked

God for the food, I made a plan.

"Grandpop," I said when he was finished with the blessing, "Can I help you feed the pigs next week?"

Grandpop put a spoonful of mashed potatoes on my plate and gave Grammy a questioning look.

"What brings this on?" he asked. "Have you decided to be a farmer?"

I searched my mind for an answer and then I decided he had already given me the perfect one.

"I don't want to be a farmer now," I said. "But when I grow up maybe I'll marry one. I should find out what it's like, don't you think?"

Grammy laughed and said, "You should definitely find out because you might not like birthing baby pigs. If I had known what I was getting into I might have married Earl Glick instead." She winked at Grandpop.

Grandpop said, "Sure, then you would be a preacher's wife. You could go to every funeral and comfort all the grieving widows."

Grammy and Grandpop continued to tease each other and I decided they had forgotten all about my request to feed the pigs. But Grandpop didn't. On Monday he woke me up early and took me out to the barn before it was even light. Being in the pig barn was as smelly as being in the chicken house, but at least we didn't have to walk through the manure. I walked alongside Grandpop, helping him dip the feed into the feeding troughs while he sang "Work for the Night is Coming."

I helped him every morning and by the end of the week I was exhausted. But when Grandpop asked me if I wanted to marry a farmer I said, "Yes." I knew if I married a preacher I would have to comfort the grieving widows. Baba was enough grieving widows to last me a lifetime.

Nadia said the chickens didn't get sick and die but she thought she was going to die from helping to feed them. She said she'd rather marry a preacher than a farmer because farmers smell bad and preachers wear fancy robes and smell like incense.

Nadia must have been daydreaming when she came to church with me because Grammy's preacher wore a straight black suit with a little bit of white collar peeping out of the top. And as far as I could tell he didn't smell like anything special.

I didn't know where Nadia got this business about robes and incense. Sometimes I thought she and I lived in two different worlds.

4

Pig Poop
and Foot Washings

"Why don't we get to wash feet?" asked Nadia.

"Shhh! I'll tell you later." I whispered, glancing around to see if everyone had heard her.

The women in the church basement didn't say a word as they took off their dark stockings. Nadia and I and other young girls sat on old church benches around the edge of the large room and watched as the women took turns sitting on the pairs of folding chairs.

Grammy sat on one of the chairs and skinny Mrs. Buckwalter knelt in front of her. The Buckwalter twins hung on to their mother's long skirt.

Grammy put her foot into the basin of water that sat between the two chairs and Mrs. Buckwalter sloshed water over Grammy's foot. Then she reached for a towel and dried it. Mrs. Buckwalter washed and dried Grammy's other foot too.

After Grammy washed Mrs. Buckwalter's feet, the two women gave each other a hug and a kiss. Even the little twins got a kiss from Grammy.

Grammy said, "God bless you, sister," and Mrs. Buckwalter said, "God bless you." They said it at exactly the same time so I figured they didn't even hear each other.

"So why couldn't we wash feet, anyway?" Nadia demanded after dinner that afternoon. She was lying on my bed and tracing her finger rapidly over the different colors in the quilt.

"Because we're not members of the church."

"What does it mean anyway?"

"You heard the preacher. Just as Jesus washed the feet of his disciples we're supposed to wash each other's feet. It's to show that we're willing to serve each other."

"Well doesn't that mean kids too?"

Nadia said that at her church kids even took communion. But she didn't care about that. She just wanted to wash feet.

"Let's do it now," she said. "Just me and you."

"But why?" I asked.

"Because silly, why should grownups get to do all the fun stuff at church? The kids have to be quiet and not move a muscle. The grownups get to wash feet and eat bread and wine. That's not fair."

"If you think that was wine, then you must be crazy. That was only grape juice," I said.

"Well grape juice is fine with me. But really I want to wash feet. We're best friends, aren't we? Shouldn't best friends serve each other?"

" I guess so. But how will we do it?"

Nadia had it all figured out. I helped her sneak the basin out from under the kitchen sink and a towel from the bathroom closet.

We decided the best place was in our hideout in the barn. It was pretty tricky getting the basin of water up the ladder but Nadia was determined and when she set her mind to do something she always got it done.

The hard part was finding a white towel and getting hot water. Nadia said it had to be a white towel because that was what they used at church. And it had to be hot water too, because she could see that the water had been steaming when the men carried it into the church basement that morning.

I said those things weren't important but Nadia said that in church things should be just a certain way.

I replied, "People look on the outward appearance but God looks on the heart."

Nadia gave me a blank look so I said that I should know, because after all I was the Mennonite wasn't I? After all, did the Orthodox church ever practice foot washing?

We almost got into a big fight but finally we came up with a plan. She would plan one foot washing service and I would plan another.

Nadia said we had to carry a Bible out to the barn too. She insisted on reading the same passage that the preacher had read in church.

Finally we were settled in the hideout of the barn with our basin, our white towel and the Bible. We found the passage in John 13 and figured out where the preacher had begun reading and where he stopped.

Nadia and I had a stool in our play house. We had a bench too. She pulled the stool up to the bench and placed the basin in between. It looked almost like the way the folding chairs were set up at church. She laid the towel on the bench and told me to sit on the stool. She solemnly washed my feet. I laughed when she dried my toes because it tickled. I laughed when I washed her feet too. How could I be solemn when I could hear the snorts of the pigs below us?

I laughed because a great idea was forming in my head. But first I had to do it Nadia's way.

She solemnly washed my feet.

When we were finished we stood and hugged and kissed each other and said "God bless you, sister" at exactly the same time.

Then we sang a hymn. Well, actually we sang "Jesus Loves Me" because we couldn't think of a grownup hymn that we both knew.

Now it was time to do it my way. With a big grin, I whispered my idea to Nadia.

"You're crazy," said Nadia. "You're crazier than Baba if you think I'm going to stick my feet in pig poop!"

"But that's the whole point," I said. "Jesus washed the disciples' feet because they wore sandals and their feet were dirty. Our feet should be dirty too. It's more meaningful if there's a reason behind it."

Nadia said she was cold enough without sticking her feet in some freezing pig manure. "After all, it is October," she said.

"Okay," I said. "We'll go to your house because the chicken houses are warm. We'll put our feet in chicken poop instead."

"Yeah," said Nadia. "Let's go spill the watering trough and make some goopy mess and put our feet in it."

The memory of Batko yelling Ukrainian swear words at Nadia hit me in the stomach when she said that. There was no way I was going to spill that water again. I could just see 10,000 chickens lying there dead from pneumonia.

"Let's just forget it," I said.

But Nadia wouldn't forget it. So we really did get into an argument. Nadia was about to go away mad but I got her good.

"Look," I said, "We agreed we would each plan a foot washing. You had your way and now I get my way. You have to because you just washed my feet and that means you'll serve me."

Nadia knew when she had lost an argument.

"Oh, all right," she said.

"Follow me," I said.

I led her down the ladder and we walked up and down the barn looking for a pig pen to climb into. All the pigs in the barn were mama pigs with their babies. Each mama had a different pen for just her family. The male pigs stayed in huts out in the fields.

"Don't dare go near that one," I said, pointing to a huge mama pig. "That pig is mean."

Suddenly every pig in the barn looked mean. All of them had babies to protect. I wasn't so sure I wanted to go through with this. I picked out a pig pen and started to climb over the wall but when I did the mama pig started coming toward me.

I got out of there fast!

"Maybe she's hungry," said Nadia.

"Of course she is," I said. "Pigs are always hungry."

Then I had an idea. "That's it! Let's feed them."

I was ready to get this over with. My bare feet were freezing and my teeth were chattering. I rushed to the barrel where Grandpop kept the pig feed. I scooped up a bucketful of the ground corn and poured it into the trough. Now the mama pig was busy eating but she was still right in front of the wall we wanted to climb over.

"Look," said Nadia. "Let's just forget it."

"No," I argued. "We're going to figure out a way. Follow me."

I climbed up on the wall and reached for the ceiling beam above me. The pigs grunted and gobbled just below. The feeding trough ran the whole length of the front wall. How was I going to get past that mama?

"Run and get more feed," I said to Nadia. "Fill up two buckets and pour them in that corner of the pig trough over there. Then get up here quick."

Nadia hesitated.

"You have to," I said. "Remember. You promised to serve me."

Nadia did it. Then she climbed up on the wall and reached for the beam over her head. I stepped down onto the empty end of the pig trough. But I never took my eyes off the huge pig down at the other end. I stepped into the thick, black, horrible poop on the floor of the pen.

"Oooh!" I squealed. "Hurry, Nadia. Get in here. It's great!"

I could tell Nadia was thinking about letting me stand there in that pig poop all by myself.

"You promised," I said. Nadia closed her eyes and lowered herself carefully onto the pig trough. She never did let go of the wall. She barely stuck her toes in the manure. Then she squealed as loudly as she could and jumped back out. She hustled right over that wall and left me there alone.

But I wasn't alone at all. When that mama pig heard Nadia squeal she turned and charged right toward me.

"Nadia! She's coming after me. Help!"

"Hurry, Rhoda! Hurry!" Nadia yelled from the other side of the wall.

I jumped onto the trough and put my hands up on the top edge of the pig pen. I thrust my stomach up onto the wall just as the pig reached me. There I was with my feet out in the air, balancing on the edge of the wall like a seesaw on its stand.

"Help me, Nadia!"

Nadia grabbed hold of me and pulled. I fell head first

into the soft dust of the barn floor. I lay there for a minute looking into the dirt and listening to the pigs snorting on the other side of that wall.

Falling didn't feel so good, but I laughed because I was sure it felt better than being in the pen with that pig. Do pigs bite? I wondered.

"Now I'll have to wash all of you," said Nadia. She helped dust me off and we climbed the ladder to the loft again. Every step I took I left pig manure on the ladder. Nadia hardly had any on her feet at all.

We washed our feet as quickly as possible and said, "Yuck, yuck," the whole time. "Yuck," said Nadia again. "I liked my way better."

"No, my way was more fun," I said through chattering teeth. "We'll never forget this. Oh, wait a minute. We forgot something."

I grabbed Nadia and gave her a big kiss on the cheek. But I was determined not to say what those women in the church said.

I thought of the wedding vows my Uncle Menno had made to his new wife. So I said, "This means I'll be your friend through sickness and health, for better or worse." I thought about the part that says "till death do us part" but decided not to say that.

Nadia must have read my mind because she said, "Well, I'll be your friend till the day I die."

I couldn't even imagine the day she died. She would be old and wrinkled like her Baba and just the thought of it scared me.

"Just don't die," I said.

5

Who Gets Baba's Soul?

It was a cold Friday morning in January when Baba died. Nadia knocked at our door at 7:00 with tears running down her face. She was out of breath from running.

"Please! Call an ambulance," she said. "Baba says the communist's big boots are stepping on her chest."

Grandpop made the phone call without asking any questions. Grammy pulled Nadia against her soft round body and told me to give her the hot chocolate she'd made for my breakfast.

Grandpop put all of us into his car and we drove back to Nadia's house. In the back seat of the car I held Nadia's hand and remembered my promise to be her friend through sickness and health, for better or worse. I never expected this to happen when I made that promise.

When we got to her house no one spoke anything but Ukrainian. Nadia didn't translate. Batko hovered over Baba who was lying on the floor. He fanned her and tried to get her to talk, but she was quieter than I'd ever seen her. Mama paced the floor, wailing and crying out in Ukrainian.

She grabbed me and Nadia and held us so tight I thought I would never breathe again.

Grandpop began to pray aloud and that made Mama cry even harder. Grammy rescued something that was burning on the kitchen stove and then she began to do the dishes.

Finally the ambulance arrived and Mama let go of me and Nadia. She rushed to the door and propped it open. She talked wildly to the ambulance driver but he didn't understand a word. Even Nadia couldn't think clearly to interpret for her.

Grandpop told them what he knew. The ambulance driver checked Baba's heart and her pulse. He looked from Mama to Batko and shook his head. Mama's wails filled the house.

Batko just grew more silent. Grandpop drove everyone except Grammy to the hospital. Grammy stayed behind to clean the kitchen and prepare stew for later.

Nadia did not wail like Mama but she cried and cried. When I looked at her red face and twisted mouth it felt like someone was twisting my insides. I wanted to run away but I kept hearing myself say "I'll be your friend for better or worse." I held Nadia's hand all day that day.

The doctor came into the waiting room and said that Baba had died almost immediately. By then Nadia was able to translate a little. But crying twisted her words so much her English sounded almost like another language.

It was lunch time before we got back home. We went straight to our house so Batko could use our phone to call Uncle Walter and Aunt Helen. He also called the Orthodox priest.

"He will tell us what to do," Batko said.

The priest didn't get there until late that night because he had to come from Baltimore. He went with the family to the funeral home and told everyone how the funeral should be.

Grammy and Grandpop didn't go to the funeral home but they sent me because Nadia and her family wanted me there.

The priest scared me almost as much as Baba did. He had a dark face and never smiled at me or Nadia once.

After the priest left the funeral home, Mama said we should all bring silver coins to tie into a handkerchief in the coffin. The coins would buy Baba's soul from the devil.

I was pretty sure Mama was wrong about buying Baba's soul. But I remembered how Baba talked to Dido even if he was dead. I didn't want to take a chance on her coming back to scream at me just because I hadn't kept her from the devil.

"I'll get some coins from my bank," I said.

Later at my house, Grammy heard me shaking my bank. I had only gotten twelve pennies and two dimes by the time she stopped me.

"It is impossible to buy off the devil," she said. "Jesus is the only one who can pay for our sins. If Baba did not accept Jesus when she was alive then you can't buy her soul now."

Grammy made me put the dimes back into the bank.

Now what was I going to do?

I ran to Nadia's house to tell her about my problem. I had made a promise to her for better or worse and I knew I had to keep it. Besides I didn't want any visits from Baba.

Mama gave me a fat white candle. "You are just like a daughter to me," she said. "Burn this for forty days. When Baba's soul departs you can blow it out."

Oh dear, how could I do that? I knew Grammy wouldn't let me burn a candle for her.

Nadia hid the candle and some matches under her coat and helped me think of a plan while she walked me home. We put the candle in our barn hideout where we had washed each other's feet. We lit the candle and Nadia crossed herself and I did too. But I didn't pray for Baba's soul. I prayed she would not come back to haunt me and that Grandpop would not find out about the candle in his barn.

On Sunday morning Grandpop solved my problem with the coin. He always gave me a quarter to put in the offering box at the back of the church. When I saw that quarter I knew what I would do.

I gave it to Batko on Sunday afternoon. I hoped it was enough. He smiled and gave me a big hug and called me his little daughter.

"Dotca, dotca," he said as he stroked my pigtails.

The funeral was early Monday morning. I had never been to a funeral at 7:00 in the morning. Baba's funeral was early because the family had to take her to Bound Brook, New Jersey to a Ukrainian cemetery. I was relieved to know Baba would be five hours away with Delaware between her and me.

In her coffin Baba looked like someone from another country. She was wearing Ukrainian clothes and a lace scarf on her head. She had a picture of Jesus in her folded hands and a strip of paper with Ukrainian words wrapped around her forehead. Nadia said the Ukrainian writing was a prayer. In the corner was the handkerchief with Nadia's coins and my quarter inside.

I had never been in Nadia's church before. I couldn't stop looking at all the strange pictures of angels and Jesus and Mary on the wall. There must have been a

He was wearing a long black robe.

hundred of them and every one was draped with an embroidered scarf. There was a thick, sweet smell in the air that I thought must come from the candles burning all around the church.

Nadia wanted me to sit with her. Mama and Batko did too, so Grammy let me. She and Grandpop sat on the back row. Well, actually we never did sit. Everyone stood for the whole service.

A door opened at the front of the church and the priest came down the aisle and walked around the coffin with Baba in it. He was wearing a long black robe with thousands of shiny gold designs woven into it. He waved a little pot he had on a chain and a cloud of smoke surrounded the coffin. Then I knew where the sweet smell was coming from.

"What's that?" I whispered to Nadia.

"Incense," she said.

I knew about incense from the Bible but I had never seen or smelled it before.

The priest had a helper who said some of the service in English but mostly it was in Ukrainian.

Actually the priest and his helper didn't exactly say anything. It was more like they sang it. The priest stood right in front of me in the aisle by the coffin. I squeezed in close to Nadia and held her hand tightly. Oh how I wished I could change places with her or better yet stand in the back between Grammy and Grandpop.

On the back of the priest's long stiff robe was a picture of Jesus. He was staring right into my face. I didn't like that, especially when the helper repeated one prayer that said, "Forgive her sins both voluntary and involuntary."

I knew it was Baba's sins they were praying for but I kept thinking about how I had stolen a quarter that was meant for God and used it to buy Baba's soul from the devil. Not only that; I was burning a candle in the barn right now and I knew Grammy and Grandpop would not approve.

I tried hard not to look at Jesus' face. The priest's Jesus looked hard and his eyes looked right into my mind. I just knew he could see that I was thinking about that candle. He didn't look at all like the picture of Jesus I had on my wall—the one with him rescuing a lost sheep from the briar bushes. My Jesus picture never made me feel all scared inside.

The fear wasn't only on the inside. It was all around me. Every time the priest shook his pot of incense the fear rose in a cloud around my head and I was sure everyone could see it.

When the service was over all the people walked by the priest. When I saw that everyone who filed by the priest also kissed the dead Baba I tried to run out of the church.

Grandpop picked me up and I didn't care if I was ten years old. I put my head on his shoulder and cried.

Nadia's family went to Bound Brook, New Jersey to bury Baba. I didn't go because Grammy said missing school on Friday was bad enough. I couldn't miss another day.

I knew I had promised to be Nadia's friend for better or worse. I couldn't think of anything worse than going to New Jersey with that priest to bury Baba. I was sure glad it was Grammy who told Nadia I couldn't go. Maybe Nadia would never find out how relieved I was.

6

Fire!

Nadia was gone to New Jersey for only one day. But she didn't come to school for a whole week. I missed her like crazy. It was the longest week of my life. And the next month was the longest month of my life. I worried every day about that candle burning in the barn.

I worried about Grandpop finding it, but mostly I worried about it catching the barn on fire. Every day after school I went to the barn to check on it.

Grandpop teased me about spending so much time in the barn these days.

"I guess you're just practicing up for when you marry a farmer," he said.

I kept a piece of paper in the hideout. Every day I made a mark on the paper to count the days. Then I put the candle on top of the paper so it wouldn't blow away.

Finally I got up to thirty days. Only ten more days to go. So far so good.

That's what I thought. That's what I thought until I saw the smoke when Nadia and I got off the school bus on the thirty-first day.

"Nadia, the barn is on fire! Hurry! Run! We have to tell Grandpop! What am I going to do? What am I going to tell Grandpop?" I cried all the way in the lane. Now Grandpop will send me home and I won't be able to play with Nadia, I thought. And what about the pigs? What if the pigs die? I could just see two hundred pigs lying black and stiff on the floor of their pens.

I didn't even hear the fire trucks coming down the lane behind me. They were blowing their horns as hard as they could and I didn't even notice until Nadia pushed me off the road.

The trucks roared right past us. I was so relieved I stopped running and sat in the road and cried.

"Maybe we should go to your house instead," I said to Nadia.

"And miss all this excitement? You've got to be out of your mind," Nadia said. "Come on, Rhoda."

"No, Nadia. Don't you understand. The fire is all my fault. My candle started the fire."

"Well then it's not your fault. It's Mama's fault for making you burn it and it's your Grammy's fault for not letting you burn it in the house. It's not your fault and I'll tell them so."

Nadia grabbed me by the hand and dragged me the rest of the way home.

As we got closer I could hear the pigs squealing. I had never heard such an awful sound before.

I could see Grammy and Grandpop standing in the driveway watching the firemen roll out their hoses. I tried to sneak around to the back door but Grammy stopped me.

Before Grammy could say a word Nadia spoke up. "It's not Rhoda's fault you know. She had to burn a candle because of Baba's soul. Mama told her to. But you

"Nadia, the barn is on fire!"

wouldn't let her give silver coins for Baba's soul so she had to hide the candle. It's not her fault."

At least that's what Nadia told me later. I was crying so bad I couldn't even listen to her. I just wanted to run to my room and never look into Grammy and Grandpop's faces again.

Grammy pulled me close to her and said, "Hush! It's not the end of the world. The firemen are putting it out."

"What about the pigs?" I sobbed.

"I think the pigs are okay," said Grammy.

Nadia was fascinated with the firemen and their great spray of water. She got as close to them as she could before Grandpop told her to come back and watch from the porch.

I didn't see what was so exciting about the firemen. I could go my whole life and never see a fireman again.

None of the pigs were hurt. But I told Grandpop I didn't think I would make a good farmer's wife. First, I had nearly killed 10,000 chickens and now I had nearly burned all Grandpop's pigs.

I didn't get any dessert for a week and I wasn't allowed to play with Nadia on Saturday or Sunday. That was the hardest part of all.

The next week there was a forty day service for Baba. Nadia begged and begged for me to go with her.

"You can come too," she told Grammy and Grandpop. "You'll just love it. After the service there's a big feast. There'll be lots of varenyky and Ukrainian pastries."

Grammy and Grandpop said we had to go to our church. But we did stop in on the way home because Mama and Batko invited them to come and eat with them.

We got there just as the service was ending. All the people were walking by the front of the church where Baba's coffin once lay. A table was covered with breads, cakes and candles. The church smelled like incense.

Aunt Helen was holding a big tray with something white in it that had cherries on top. Everyone took a spoonful of the white stuff when they walked by. I thought it was like when the grownups at church had communion until Nadia told me later the white stuff was rice.

"Why do you eat rice?" I asked her.

Nadia shrugged. "I don't know. Because Baba died I guess."

"Well lots of people die but I don't see their families eating rice," I said.

Nadia said I should ask the priest if I wanted to know. But suddenly I didn't want to know anymore.

I sat with Grammy and Grandpop at the meal. Mama and Aunt Helen and other women from the church served the meal. But they wouldn't let Grammy help because she was their guest.

There was chicken and varenyky and potato salad, and all kinds of other foods. Some of the men drank vodka but Grandpop didn't have any.

I thought maybe that would offend Batko but he still talked to Grandpop and told him how happy he was that we had come.

"Rhoda is just like my daughter," he said. "She is away from her home now so I will be her Batko." He patted me on the head and called me his dotca. Then he dished me a big helping of cake. I was so full I thought I would get sick but I ate it anyway because I knew Batko only wanted to make me happy.

7

Rhoda Goes to Bound Brook

After a cold, rainy winter Nadia and I were so glad when spring finally came. We were anxious to get back to our kingdom. It would be different now, of course, because the wicked Baba was no longer around to be our enemy. Still we didn't return to the kingdom until all the leaves had grown back on the weeping willow branches. We didn't want anyone to know where it was.

One day in April I said, "Maybe all the leaves will be back in time for Easter. We can hide Easter eggs in the branches of the tree. Easter is only a week away, you know."

"No," said Nadia. "Batko said just last night that Easter is two weeks from now."

"Well, Grammy said Easter is next Sunday and my mom and dad are coming to see us on Friday so I know she's right."

"But I know Batko is right because he said we go to Bound Brook in three weeks to visit Baba's grave. He said we have to do that one week after Easter."

"You don't think my mom and dad would come to

visit if it weren't a holiday do you? My dad has to work, you know. What are you talking about, visiting Baba's grave?"

"It's a tradition. We go to the Ukrainian cemetery and put food on the graves of our loved ones."

"Food? You mean like real food? Whatever for?"

"Because, it's for their journey?"

"What journey?"

"For after they die. Don't you understand anything?" Nadia rolled her eyes in disgust at my ignorance. That made me mad.

"I think I understand a lot more than you do," I said.

"Well, did your Grammy die?" asked Nadia.

I had to admit I didn't really know anyone who had died. I decided not to argue with her.

"What kind of food do you give them?" I asked.

"Easter bread," said Nadia. "Easter bread and Easter eggs."

I didn't know what Easter bread was. I knew what Easter eggs were, though. Grammy said she didn't think I should color eggs because they have nothing to do with the real meaning of Easter. I told her Mom helped us color Easter eggs every year and she just said, "Sometimes I wonder if your mother forgot her upbringing."

Then she said I should just wait until my parents arrived to see what they would say about dyeing eggs.

I was excited about seeing Mom and Dad and my baby brother. It was hard to believe I actually had a baby brother because I only saw him right after he was born and at Christmas time.

Thinking about Christmas reminded me of something.

"Hey Nadia," I said. "Remember Christmas? We celebrated before you did. You didn't have Christmas until January. Maybe it's the same with Easter."

Nadia said, "Let's go ask Mama or Batko."

Mama was in the garden with Batko. They were getting the ground ready for planting. Nadia asked about Easter and she told us to look on the calendar in the kitchen.

The calendar didn't prove anything to me because I couldn't read a word of it with its strange Ukrainian letters. Nadia found another one in her parent's bedroom. It was an advertisement for the feed store down the road and it was in English.

We took both of them to the garden. The English calendar showed Easter one week earlier than the Ukrainian calendar. Batko said that the Orthodox church uses the Julian calendar, which is different from the calendar other people use. I had never heard of such a thing but it settled our argument about Easter.

Batko asked me if I was going to Bound Brook with his family and I said I wasn't.

"Yes, you are," he said. "You are one of the family. Baba loved you so. She would want you to."

I was pretty sure Baba never loved me. And if she wanted me to be there I didn't know if I should go or stay.

Nadia really wanted me to go along.

"It'll be loads of fun," she said. "We have to leave early in the morning and we get to eat in a restaurant along the way. And after we get there we tend the graves and have a picnic. There are lots of Ukrainians dressed in Ukrainian clothes and you will just love it! Please say you'll go."

"Well, I'll ask Grammy and Grandpop," I said.

I thought maybe eating in a restaurant would make the rest of the trip worthwhile.

Grammy said since it was on a Sunday I would miss church and she didn't know about that. But Nadia told her there was a huge church at the cemetery and we would go to a service there.

"And not only that," she said, "But a priest comes right to the graves to say a prayer."

I almost changed my mind when I heard about the priest. But Nadia said it would not be the same one that comes to her church.

Nadia and her family were determined that I would go. Batko came over to give a special invitation. Grandpop couldn't turn him down. He really liked Batko and Batko liked him.

Grandpop even said he'd feed Batko's chickens for him on that day. Batko smiled a huge smile and said, "Just like family."

Uncle Walter and Aunt Helen came to visit the day before we left for Bound Brook. Aunt Helen was carrying a basket of beautiful eggs she had painted. She gave one to everyone, including me.

"Teach us to make pysanky too," Nadia begged Aunt Helen.

Aunt Helen agreed, and Nadia and I followed her into the kitchen. She pulled a little wooden tool and a ball of dark wax from her travel bag, then got some eggs from Mama's refrigerator. She showed Nadia and I how to heat the tool with the candle and scoop wax into the tool. Then she helped us draw designs on the eggs.

"See," said Aunt Helen. "You dip the egg in the yellow dye and when it's dry you draw more wax designs on it. Then you dip it into the orange dye."

We kept doing that until we'd used all the colors.

"Now hold it close to the candle and let the wax melt," said Aunt Helen. "Wipe it with this cloth until all the wax is gone and you can see the different colors. Look what beautiful pysanky you made!"

Ours weren't as beautiful as Aunt Helen's, of course, but we thought they were perfect.

We all squeezed into Uncle Walter's car early the next morning before it was even light. It was chilly and I was sleepy so I went right back to sleep in the car.

I ordered pancakes with syrup at the restaurant. It was a long skinny silver restaurant that looked like a train car. There was a machine that played music. Helen kept giving me and Nadia nickels to put in the machine, so we listened to Elvis Presley music the whole time we ate.

Nadia was right about the church in Bound Brook. It was the biggest building I had ever seen and on the top of it were golden spires like the churches in magazine. I didn't even have time to be scared of the priests. I was so busy looking at all the gold and pictures inside.

When the service was over we went back to the car to get the things for the grave. Mama asked me to carry the basket with the paska. The paska was the special Easter bread with icing on top. It smelled so good I could hardly wait for the picnic.

Nadia and Aunt Helen carried pots of flowers. The men carried a shovel and grass clippers. We walked single file through the cemetery.

Back home in Pennsylvania, my friends and I sometimes wandered through the graveyard at our church but I'd never seen anything like this. There were huge shiny grave stones with strange Ukrainian writing on them.

The names on the gravestones at my church all sounded like family names—Landis, Kulp, Clemmer or Hackman. I couldn't read any of these names.

Nadia and I ran through the grass.

Nadia pranced up the path ahead of us. Then she twirled around and said, "Isn't this just the most fun in the whole world?"

Batko scolded her because she almost ran into an old lady who was walking with a cane.

It was a long walk and we saw many people along the way. Everyone was speaking Ukrainian. I thought Nadia and I must be the only people there who spoke English.

Finally we came to Baba's grave. There were two shiny gravestones. Why are there two of them, I wondered.

I set the paska down in the grass where Mama pointed.

"Who else died?" I asked Nadia

"Dido, Baba's husband," she said.

"But I thought he died in the concentration camp. How did he get over here?"

"He's not really here," said Nadia. "Baba bought this plot for him a long time ago. She said he would join her here when she died. She said he couldn't bear to be away from her."

"Oh," I said.

I guessed that was why she always thought Dido was sitting in the green chair at Nadia's house.

Nadia wanted to run around and look at the other graves. She said there were some really neat statues she wanted to show me. Walter and Batko were trimming the grass around Dido and Baba's graves and Mama and Helen were planting flowers. Mama said we could go but not to stay away too long.

Nadia pulled me by the hand up and down the long rows of the cemetery. There was a warrior statue, images of Jesus cut into the gravestones and lots of statues of Mary.

Nadia and I found a statue we both loved the best. It was a white one of a little girl angel holding a bunch of flowers. A real ribbon around her neck fluttered in the wind. Nadia said probably a young girl had died.

"If I would die young I would want a statue just like that one," Nadia said. "I especially would want a white ribbon around my neck. Don't you just love the way it blows in the wind? It almost looks like she's not a statue at all but a real live person.

Nadia stood there with her hair blowing in the wind and the sun on her face and I just knew she would not die young so I told her so.

Then we heard Batko calling our names. We turned to go and as we did we passed old women working alone over the graves of their husbands. We passed whole families planting flowers on the graves of someone they loved. I couldn't help wondering who had died in each of those graves.

Baba and Dido's graves were neat and pretty when we got back. Mama had saved two marigolds for me and Nadia.

Nadia said, "You plant one for Dido since I don't really remember him anyway. Will you be mad if I plant the one for Baba?"

"That's a good idea," I said.

Dido didn't scare me so much now that Baba was dead. Maybe Dido never did scare me. Maybe it was only Baba who scared me. I didn't know for sure.

A priest came to the grave and said prayers for Baba and Dido. It was all in Ukrainian and I didn't understand a word of it. When the service was over all the people walked by the priest and kissed a cross he held out to them. I did too. I looked at Nadia's braids and then at my own and thought, I bet he doesn't even know I'm not Ukrainian.

Then we had a picnic. Mama and Aunt Helen had prepared lots of food. We sat on a blanket in the grass and stuffed ourselves with fried chicken and pastries.

The grownups drank vodka to salute the dead. Nadia and I took off our shoes and ran barefoot in the grass.

I told Nadia she was right. It had been a fun day!

8

Please Don't Go

When I came back from Bound Brook with Nadia's family we only had five more weeks of school. My family was expecting me to come home as soon as school was out. Mom was strong again and she missed me. I missed her too.

But I couldn't just leave Nadia. She was my best friend—better than my friend Beth whom I'd gone to school and Sunday School with since first grade.

Nadia was mad when she realized I would be leaving.

"What do you mean, you're going home to live?" she demanded. "You can't leave me. I don't have any other friends."

"But you can make friends," I said. "As long as you remember I'm your best friend."

"I can't make new friends. You're the only one who ever wanted to be my friend. I don't like any of those other people."

I didn't know what I wanted. When I chose Nadia to be my friend I only thought about having someone to love me for one year. I didn't realize I would love her forever.

"Maybe Grammy and Grandpop will let me stay," I said.

We ran to ask them.

"If it were up to me you could stay here until you marry your farmer," Grandpop said. "But you do have parents and this has always been a temporary arrangement, you know."

"But my Batko will be her Batko too," insisted Nadia.

"Please can we call her mom and dad and ask them?"

Nadia begged to use the phone. Grammy let her.

My mom listened to Nadia's pleading and then she asked to speak to Grammy. When Grammy hung up we still didn't have an answer.

"Your mom wants to talk to your father about it," she said.

The next day Mom called us back.

"Rhoda, we're ready for you to come home. Your friends miss you and you have a baby brother you hardly know."

I didn't know what to say or feel. In a way I did want to go home. But in another way I wanted to stay with Nadia and play in the willow kingdom and go to the ocean in the summer time with her.

Mom said she and Dad had decided I could stay until early August and then I would have to come home to get ready for the new school year.

Nadia was so happy she hugged me and jumped up and down at the same time.

We had two more months together. We filled them with wonderful things: wading in the creek, making hideouts under the porch, ruling our willow kingdom and having picnics everyday at lunch time.

Grammy and Mama seemed to know we needed every minute together. They didn't make us do many chores and they always made delicious foods for our picnics.

I went to Ocean City with Nadia and Mama and Batko. I'd never been to the ocean before. We jumped in the waves and choked on the salty water and squealed when we were sure it was a crab that brushed against our toes.

Mama and Batko sat under a beach umbrella and laughed at us. Then they took us to the boardwalk. We rode a roller coaster and a ferris wheel. A photographer took our picture and put it in a little telescope so we could see ourselves with our sand castle when we held it up to the light.

But my favorite part of all was the ride on the huge merry-go-round. It had different kinds of animals and I chose a pig with a ear of corn carved on its side. I told Nadia to ride the rooster because of her Batko's chickens. But she said chickens were boring. She rode a sea dragon instead.

August came before we were ready. But we were never going to be ready. On our last night together Nadia slept over at Grammy's house with me. We reminded ourselves of all the fun things we'd done together. We made a list and promised each other we would never do them with anyone else.

I didn't know how I was ever going to join the church if I couldn't wash feet with anyone beside Nadia. So we agreed we would never do it the pig manure way with anyone else.

"And another thing," said Nadia, "when you grow up and have children I want you to name the first one after me."

I promised her I would and she said her first girl would be named Rhoda for sure.

Dad held my baby brother.

The next day was just terrible. I was anxious to see Mom and Dad but I knew when they came my time with Nadia would be almost over.

When we saw their station wagon coming in Grandpop's lane Nadia grabbed me by the hand and dragged me to the woods behind the barn.

"Run!" she said. "Don't let them see you."

But I broke away from her and raced into Mom's arms. The smell of her shampoo and the sound of her voice made me feel how good it would be to go home again.

Dad held my baby brother and I hugged them both at the same time. I could hardly believe that baby and I belonged in the same family.

Mom and Dad stayed for the weekend so Nadia and I had a day and a half to play together. Nadia went to Grammy's church with me even though there was a service at her church.

Batko and Mama were invited for Sunday dinner. We had all my favorite foods—corn on the cob and pork roast with cabbage and potatoes. The adults ate because their hearts weren't breaking. But Nadia and I didn't eat much at all.

When it was time for me to leave, Nadia's face was all twisted like when Baba died and my insides were twisted just the same way.

Batko pulled me close in a big hug and his eyes filled with tears. "Little dotca," he said in Ukrainian. I didn't need Nadia to translate it for me. I had heard it so many times before.

Mama pushed a bag of Ukrainian pastries into my hands and said to eat them on the trip. But she would not look at me.

"Please don't take her away from me," Nadia begged

my parents. "Please let her stay just one more year." My parents shook their heads gently because they knew one more year would never be enough. Then they surprised us.

"If it's alright with Grammy and Grandpop she can come back next summer," they said.

That promise was the only thing that made our good-bye bearable. I will always remember the way Nadia looked through the back window of Daddy's car, leaning toward me and waving. I could tell from her face that she was already planning for next summer.

Kristen Keeler Goes to Bound Brook Too

Kristen carried the basket with the Easter bread out to the car.

"Put it on the floor behind the front seat," called her mother from the porch. "I'll get the basket of eggs."

"Oh no," said Kristen. "I want to get the eggs too. Can I Mother? Please?"

Mother laughed. "Sure, but what am I going to bring?"

"You can bring the suitcases," said Kristen.

So Mother went upstairs and carried down the suitcases. She carried both hers and Kristen's out to the car. Then she went back in and got her straw hat, the one with the white scarves attached. She put the hat on the front seat.

"Now it's time for the gardening things," said Mother.

"Oh, I want to put the watering can in," said Kristen. "And the marigolds too. You can get the other things."

So Mother put in the hedge trimmers, the trowels and the fertilizer that smelled like dead fish. She put in some old fashioned grass clippers too. "I think that's just about everything we'll need," she said. "Let's go inside and say goodbye to Daddy and baby Jonathan."

Daddy was changing Jonathan's diaper. Jonathan was crying as loudly as he could.

"I know why he's crying," said Kristen. "He's sad because he's not going to Bound Brook, New Jersey with Mother and me. Don't you wish you were going, Daddy?"

Daddy finished diapering Jonathan and said, "Well, I think Jonathan and I are going to have a great time at home. But I am going to miss my two favorite girls."

He picked up Kristen and gave her a big hug. "Now you take good care of your mother," he said. "Don't let her fall asleep while she's driving, you hear?"

Kristen kissed her father and wiggled out of his arms. "Let's go!" she said.

The family followed Kristen out to the car. Daddy kissed everyone again and Kristen told Jonathan to take good care of Daddy. Then she and her mother left for Bound Brook, New Jersey.

Kristen picked up her mother's straw hat and put it on her head. She threw the scarves over her shoulders the way she had seen Mother do it.

"I'm sure glad you changed your mind about taking me to Bound Brook with you," she said to her mother. "But why are we going to New Jersey? Is it to put food and flowers on Baba's grave? I thought you didn't like Baba."

"Yes, Kristen," said her mother. "We'll put flowers on Baba's grave. But there's more to the story. Maybe I should tell you the rest of the story right now."

9

I'll Be Your Friend Till the Day I Die

Nadia and I became letter writers the year we were in sixth grade. She wrote and said that sometimes she had lunch with a new girl at school. She was trying to decide if they could be good friends.

I wrote and told her Beth and I were buddies again but I would never wash feet with her.

When May came I could hardly wait for school to be out. We wrote every week in May describing all the things we would do together. Finally the day came when I could go to Maryland again.

We spent the summer doing all the things we'd done before and a few more besides. We slept out in the willow kingdom. We dressed up in Ukrainian clothes and pretended Batko's manure spreader was the ship that brought us to America.

Nadia and I spent every summer together after that. Usually I stayed at Grammy and Grandpop's but one summer her parents even let her come to live with me in Pennsylvania.

Even going to high school didn't change our friendship. Nothing was ever going to change our friendship. We had promised to be friends for better or for worse.

Two worse things happened to us when we were in high school.

First my brother was in an accident. For three days we thought he was going to die. Nadia's Mama and Batko brought her to see me and she sat with me in the hospital until the doctors said he would live. Nadia held my hand just like when we were little girls and Baba was dead. My insides felt just the way they had then.

Then when we were in the eleventh grade, Nadia's Mama died from bone cancer. The twisted insides were starting to feel very familiar.

I couldn't go to her funeral but Daddy drove me to Bound Brook, New Jersey for the tending of the graves at Easter time.

It didn't seem fair that Nadia's mama should die. I had never lost anyone and here Nadia was planting flowers on her Dido's, Baba's, and Mama's graves.

We walked around the graveyard looking at all the statues and remembering our favorite ones. We saved the one of the little girl angel until last. The ribbon around her neck was gray and torn.

Nadia said, "When I die, please keep a fresh ribbon around the neck of my statue."

She seemed so serious and sad that I didn't even try to argue with her. I knew she wasn't going to die but I said I'd bring her a fresh ribbon every year.

On that day we talked about our plans for the future. We talked about college and how we'd always planned to be roommates. Nadia said now that Mama was dead she didn't know if she could go away from home and leave her Batko alone.

I couldn't even imagine college without Nadia.

By the end of our senior year, we'd decided to go to

The ribbon around her neck was gray and torn.

Salisbury State in Salisbury, Maryland. It was close to her home and the two of us would live with Batko and save on expenses.

I arrived at Nadia's place the day after I graduated. We were excited about life. We both had jobs in Ocean City. She was going to sell telescope pictures on the beach and I had a waitressing job at one of the good restaurants in town. We were serious about earning money for college.

But not too serious to have a good time. By now, we were both interested in boys. Nadia met a lot of guys on her job. Especially lifeguards.

She was crazy about one of the lifeguards named Chip. He liked her too and the two of them wanted me to meet Chip's friend, Larry. Finally Nadia and I both had a day off on the same day.

Larry and Chip decided to take us boating down to Assateague Island. We met them at the harbor at ten o'clock in the morning. The sun was hot and the weather was perfect. We had packed picnic baskets and the guys had brought drinks.

Except for being nervous about Larry, I was feeling just great. This was my first real boat ride and I loved the speed and the wind in my hair.

Nadia and I were wearing matching hats we had bought on the boardwalk. They were straw hats with white scarves attached to tie them on. We both looked gorgeous in those hats and we knew it.

We put down anchor in a desolate stretch of Assateague Island. Chip turned on his transistor radio. We opened the picnic basket and the guys brought out the drinks. I hadn't thought about them bringing beer. It was the only drink they brought. I couldn't believe they didn't have a single soda. And here I was stuck on a quiet island with them.

Nadia said I should just relax and have a beer. I thought about the vodka her Batko drank. To her it was no big deal. But my church didn't even drink real wine for communion.

I finally tried the beer because I was so thirsty. I hated the taste of it. I think Nadia did too, but she didn't let Chip see it.

The guys made up for what we didn't drink. I could tell this wasn't their first beer. I didn't like how it made me feel to see them drinking. For some reason the fear in my stomach reminded me of Baba's funeral. I sat there on the beach with my friends laughing and joking around me. I stared into the gently lapping water and remembered the smell of incense.

Larry tugged at my arm, saying the four of us were going to go walking on the beach. I shook the smell of incense from my head and followed. We picked up whelk shells that had been washed in by spring storms. Late in the afternoon we headed home.

Nadia was having a great time and I could see how crazy she was about Chip. He drove the boat and she sat in a seat up front beside him. I had loved the speed in the morning but now Chip seemed to be driving faster than before. He kept looking at Nadia while he drove.

I couldn't blame him. She was beautiful with her dark hair and the sparkle in her eyes. She held her hat down with one hand so it wouldn't blow away. The wind whipped the white scarves around her head and carried her laughter out across the bay.

I guess that is how I will always remember her. It was the last time I ever saw my beloved Nadia.

Neither she nor Chip saw the boat that hit us. They were having such a good time with each other that they didn't even know they were in danger.

One minute I saw Nadia's laughing eyes and the next thing I knew I was in a hospital bed. I had been in a coma for weeks. My mom was at my bedside when I woke up.

When I asked for Nadia she whispered "Hush. Later we'll talk about Nadia. Right now you need to get better."

They couldn't keep Nadia's death a secret. I asked for her every day and when they avoided my questions I knew the truth.

I didn't need them to tell me anything. Whenever I closed my eyes I saw Nadia with the scarves of her hat flapping in the wind. And when I opened them I could still see that image.

Only it wasn't Nadia's face anymore. Now it was the face of a little girl angel. The white ribbon around her neck fluttered in the breeze.

The ribbon was bright and clean because I had promised to change it every year.

Kristen Keeler and the Angel with Pigtails

Kristen carried the Easter bread and the basket of colored eggs from the car to the cemetery. Her mother carried the gardening things. It was a big load for both of them but somehow they did it.

The sun was shining. A breeze whipped the white scarves of Mother's straw hat gently around Kristen's head. Mother and Kristen crossed a bridge over a wide stream. The bridge took them to a cemetery. Everywhere there were people carrying flowers and baskets of food.

Everywhere there were huge shiny gravestones with statues and strange crosses. All around her Kristen could see people cleaning up around the gravestones.

A priest walked by in his long robe and a strange hat. Kristen stepped to the other side of the path until he went by. Then she turned to see if there was a picture of Jesus on the back of his robe. But there wasn't.

"Am I going too fast?" her mother asked.

"No, I'm coming. I just wanted to see that priest for a minute."

"We're almost there," Mother said.

It seemed like a long way, but there was so much to look at that Kristen didn't care.

"Mother, look! Is that woman wearing Ukrainian clothes?"

"Yes, isn't that embroidery beautiful?"

"But why is she reading a book in the cemetery?"

"Maybe she's waiting for someone else to come. Maybe she just wants to sit for a while with the one who died."

"Oh," said Kristen.

Just then Mother set down her basket. She ran right into the outstretched arms of an old man with gray hair.

"Batko! It's so good to see you."

The old man stroked Mother's hair and called her his dotca.

Kristen didn't need anyone to tell her what it meant.

When Mother introduced Batko to Kristen he smiled and tears filled his eyes.

"Dotca," he said.

Kristen smiled and called him Batko. But Batko said she should call him Dido.

"Dido means Grandpa," he said.

"Where are Walter and Helen?" Mother asked Batko.

Batko said he was waiting for them.

There were four shiny gravestones. The one on the end had a statue of a little girl angel.

"Mother!" exclaimed Kristen. "Nadia's angel wears pigtails!"

"Yes," said Mother. "Aren't they beautiful?"

Suddenly Uncle Walter and Aunt Helen were there. They hugged and kissed everyone and Aunt Helen kissed Kristen on both cheeks. Then she took a Ukrainian egg from the basket she had brought.

"A pysanky for you," she said handing it to Kristen.

"Did you really paint it yourself? I wish I could do that."

Kristen watered the flowers.

"Well, you should get your mother to show you how. I know she knows, because I showed her," said Aunt Helen.

"I know. She told me," said Kristen.

Uncle Walter, Aunt Helen and Mother planted flowers on the graves. They pulled weeds and trimmed the high grasses.

Batko showed Kristen the water faucet nearby and the two of them filled the watering can.

Kristen watered the flowers.

"Did you see the willow tree your mama planted for Nadia?" Batko said to Kristen.

Kristen looked at the tree with its long branches that swished in the breeze. The branches were like a curtain that hung over Nadia's grave.

"Just like the willow kingdom," Kristen said.

"Almost," Mother whispered.

After a while a priest came and said prayers. Kristen clung tightly to her mother's hand and watched as the cloud of incense rose gently around the statue of the little angel. Batko kissed the cross with Jesus on it. Aunt Helen and Uncle Walter did too. Kristen waited to see what Mother would do. When mother kissed the cross, Kristen did too. The cross was cold on her lips and Kristen shivered. She thought about the picture of Jesus in her Bible, the one with the sheep in his arms, and then she smiled into the sun.

The priest left and Aunt Helen spread a blanket under the willow tree. Batko peeked through her baskets and nibbled on the delicious Ukrainian food Helen had brought.

When Mother thought no one was looking she untied the old ribbon from the statue of the little girl. She pulled a shiny white one out of her pocket.

But Kristen was watching. "Can I have the old one?" she asked.

Mother handed her the old ribbon and tied the new one around the neck of the statue. Then she kissed the little girl angel. The ribbon fluttered in the breeze.

"Come and eat," called Helen.

Kristen tasted everything—the ham, the varenyky, and even the fried bread stuffed with chicken livers. But she liked the Ukrainian pastries the best of all.

When she was full she leaned back on the blanket and looked up into the branches of the willow tree. Then she had an idea.

Kristen climbed the tree.

"Can I climb the tree too?" a voice asked from below.

Kristen looked down to see who was speaking. It was a girl about her size. The girl didn't wait for an answer. She just climbed into the tree.

The little girl's parents were under the tree talking to Batko in a foreign language.

"Are you Ukrainian?" Kristen asked.

"Yes, of course. Aren't you?"

"No, silly. I'm Mennonite."

"What's that?"

Kristen just shrugged her shoulders because, after all, if she weren't a Mennonite she wouldn't understand.

"We could still be friends," she said softly. "Let's pretend this is a willow kingdom."

"Okay," said the little girl. "And I'll be the queen."

Kristen looked at Mother and then at the angel statue. With the ribbon fluttering around its neck it almost looked like a real girl.

"I have a better idea," she whispered. "See the angel with the pigtails? Her name is Nadia. Let's let Nadia be the queen."

Questions and Activities

To think about and discuss

1. Why was Rhoda was so eager to become friends with Nadia?

2. How were the two girls alike? Name at least three ways they were different.

3. Why didn't Rhoda's Grammy and Grandpop know Batko and Mama even though they had been neighbors for years?

4. Why is it sometimes difficult to make friends with others who speak a different language or dress differently?

5. Did Grammy and Grandpop and Batko and Mama find that they had some things in common? What were they? How did Nadia and Rhoda help the grown-ups overcome their fears?

6. In what ways did the two families show friendship to each other?

7. Does it feel scary to try new foods? Can you name a food that you like now that you were once afraid to try?

8. Why did both Rhoda and Nadia know about the sufferings of their ancestors? Why do people need to talk about sad things that happened to them or their families? How might remembering help us?

9. Why did Nadia's family come to the United States? Rhoda's people also immigrated to America from Europe but that was before even her parents were born. What do you think their reasons might have been for coming to the United States?

10. Nadia was Ukrainian Orthodox and Rhoda was Mennonite. What were some of the unusual things each learned about the other's church? Were they comfortable or uncomfortable with the things they experienced in each others' churches?

11. Friendship usually involves some risks. In what ways did Nadia and Rhoda take risks when they became friends?

12. At the end of their first school year together Rhoda realized that making friends also means you can lose them. In what ways did she and Nadia keep their friendship strong even though Rhoda went back home to Pennsylvania?

13. What promises did Rhoda and Nadia make to each other in this story? Did they keep their promises?

14. When Rhoda was a grown woman she told the story

of her friendship with Nadia to her daughter, Kristen. In what ways did that friendship affect her after she was grown?

Projects you can do

1. Kristen's mother (Rhoda) travels to the Ukrainian cemetary in Bound Brook, New Jersey every year. Find Bound Brook on a map of the eastern United States. (A Ukrainian cemetary actually exists in South Bound Brook, New Jersey, but this town is small and not found on many maps.)

2. The story of Rhoda and Nadia's friendship takes place in Snow Hill, Maryland. Find Snow Hill on the map. Using the scale of miles, find the distance between Snow Hill and Bound Brook.

3. Locate Ukraine on a world map. Using an encyclopedia find out what you can about Ukraine—its history, its people, and life in Ukraine today. Watch the newspapers and other news reports for stories about Ukraine.

4. Dido, Nadia's grandfather, had been killed in a concentration camp in Siberia. Find Siberia on a world map. Use your library to find out what you can about Siberia and about the concentration camps that used to be there.

5. Visit an Orthodox church and a Mennonite church. Attend a worship service or ask the priest or pastor to give you a tour at another time. Write down some ways the churches are different and some ways they are the

same. If you go to church, how are the Mennonite and Orthodox churches different from your church? How are they similar?

6. Rhoda's ancestors lived in Europe and were persecuted for their beliefs about 400 years ago. They were called Anabaptists. Using your library or by writing to the Mennonite Information Center (see address on page 95) see what you can learn about Anabaptists. What were some of the Anabaptists' beliefs that they were willing to die for?

7. Both Nadia's and Rhoda's ancestors immigrated to America. Many immigrants came into the country through a place in New York called Ellis Island. Use your library to learn more about Ellis Island.

8. Interview your parents or grandparents to find out more about your family history. Ask about the places they lived, the churches they attended, their favorite foods, and holiday celebrations. Make a family history booklet with the information you find. Include recipes, family photos, maps, stories, and pictures which show what your family history was like.

9. Ask a parent or another grownup to describe a special friendship they had when they were young. Did they stay in touch with the friend? Why or why not?

Favorite recipes enjoyed by Nadia and Rhoda

Shoofly pie

Preheat oven to 375 degrees. Combine the following in a saucepan, bring to a boil, and set aside to cool:

1/2	cup corn syrup or molasses
1/4	cup water

Combine the following. Use two knives or a pastry cutter to cut in the shortening.

1 1/3	cup flour
1/8	teaspoon salt
2/3	cups sugar
1/4	cup shortening

Set aside 1/3 cup of this crumb mixture. Combine 1/2 cup water and 1/4 cup corn syrup. Bring to a boil. Add 1/4 teaspoon baking soda and mix into large crumb mixture. This is the batter.

Pour cooled syrup mixture into a pie crust (find a recipe for pie crust or use a frozen ready-made crust). Pour batter over syrup. On top, sprinkle the crumbs you set aside. Bake for one hour.

Piroschky

2	cups flour
1	teaspoon baking powder
1	teaspoon salt

1   tablespoon lard or margarine
1/2   cup milk
1/2   cup cream
1   egg

Sift the dry ingredients. Use two knives or a pastry cutter to cut in the lard. Add slightly beaten eggs, milk, and cream. Roll out on floured board. (If it is too sticky, add a bit of flour.) Cut into 4-inch squares. Place a mound of fresh fruit (any kind) in the center of each square. Fold opposite corners together. Pinch the edges tightly all around to prevent leaking. Bake at 400 degrees for 25 minutes.

Art Projects

Paper pysanky

You will need:

- heavy art paper
- wax crayons
- scissors
- pencil

Cut an egg shape out of paper and color it with bright crayons in different designs. Cover the bright colors completely with black crayon. Use a pencil to draw designs on the egg revealing the colors beneath.

Pysanky

You will need:

- an adult to help you
- a hard boiled egg
- colored wax
- 2 paint brushes (one with pointed tip and one with flat bristles)
- 3 containers of acrylic craft paint
- newspaper to protect your work space

1. Melt the wax by putting it in an empty soup can and setting it inside a pan of water. Heat slowly on stove until wax melts.

2. Dip the thin paint brush into the melted wax. Paint designs on the egg.

3. Use the flat brush to cover the entire egg with the lightest color of paint. Let the paint dry.

4. Use the melted wax and thin brush to add more designs.

5. Cover the egg all over with the next lightest color of paint. Let it dry.

6. Add more wax designs on the egg.

7. Cover the egg one last time with the last color of paint. Let it dry.

8. Using a spoon, dip the egg into hot water. Gently wipe the melting wax off your egg.

You have made a beautiful pysanky!

For more information about Mennonites
and Ukrainian Orthodox Christians contact:

Mennonite Information Center
2209 Millstream Rd.
Lancaster, PA 17602-1494
(717) 299-0954

The Ukrainian Museum
203 Second Avenue
New York, NY 10003
(212) 228-0110